D0442089

# Castles

Stephanie Turnbull

Designed by Laura Parker

Illustrated by Colin King

Additional illustrations by Adam Larkum
Castle consultant: Dr. Abigail Wheatley
Reading consultant: Alison Kelly

# Contents

3 High on a hill

4 A huge home

6 Types of castles

8 The keep

10 Castle life

12 Fun and games

14 Hunting

16 In the kitchen

18 Fabulous feasts

20 Knights

22 At a joust

24 Attack!

26 Fighting back

28 Castles in ruins

30 Glossary

31 Websites to visit

32 Index

# High on a hill

The ruins of a huge stone castle stand on a hill. Hundreds of years ago, this castle was full of people.

Some castles were built on cliffs, so they had a good view out to sea.

# A huge home

Castles were built for rich people such as lords and ladies or kings and queens.

Servants worked and lived in the castle grounds.

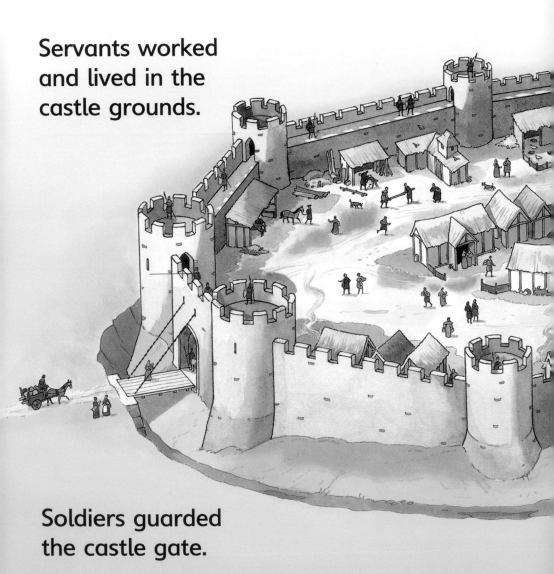

Soldiers guarded the castle gate.

4

The castle's main tower is called a keep.

A thick wall was built to keep enemies out.

Rich people had two or three castles. If they were tired of one, they moved to another.

# Types of castles

Some castles were made of wood. The keep was built on a high mound of earth.

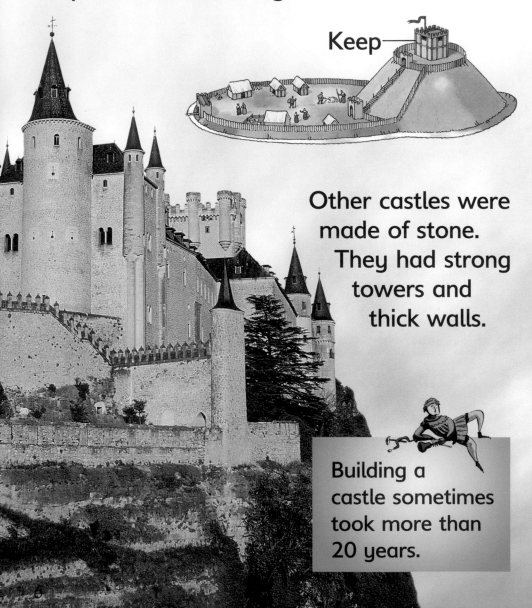

Keep

Other castles were made of stone. They had strong towers and thick walls.

Building a castle sometimes took more than 20 years.

Some castles had water around them. This is called a moat. The moat helped to keep out enemies.

People crossed the moat on a wooden platform called a drawbridge.

The drawbridge was pulled up with chains if an enemy came near.

# The keep

There were lots of rooms inside the keep.
The best rooms belonged to the lord and his family.

A bedroom

Great
Hall

Chapel

Guard room

Storeroom

A castle toilet was just a hole in the floor. Underneath was a chute that led to a pit outside.

Castles were always full of rats. Can you spot ten rats in the keep?

# Castle life

Castle owners lived in comfortable rooms. They slept in big, soft beds like this red one.

Curtains around the bed kept them snug and warm.

Servants had to sleep on the hard, cold floor.

People in castles got up early. Sometimes a bell was rung at dawn to wake everyone.

Stone castles could be damp and chilly.
Huge fires helped to keep rooms warm.

People had baths in big wooden tubs.
Servants heated the water over a fire.

Castles were noisy places. Servants worked,
children played games and dogs barked.

11

# Fun and games

There were no televisions in castle times. People had to find other things to do.

Acrobats often visited castles to put on shows.

Jugglers juggled balls or knives.

Musicians sang songs and played instruments.

Many castles had a jester. His job was to tell jokes and make everyone laugh.

This picture was painted about 700 years ago. It shows a group of musicians playing tunes for a king.

13

# Hunting

Lords and ladies enjoyed hunting.
Birds called falcons were trained to hunt.
Here are four stages of training a falcon.

1. The falcon got used to being carried and fed.

2. It was kept on a rope, and flew after bits of food.

3. Later, the falcon was able to fly freely.

4. It killed small birds and came back to its owner.

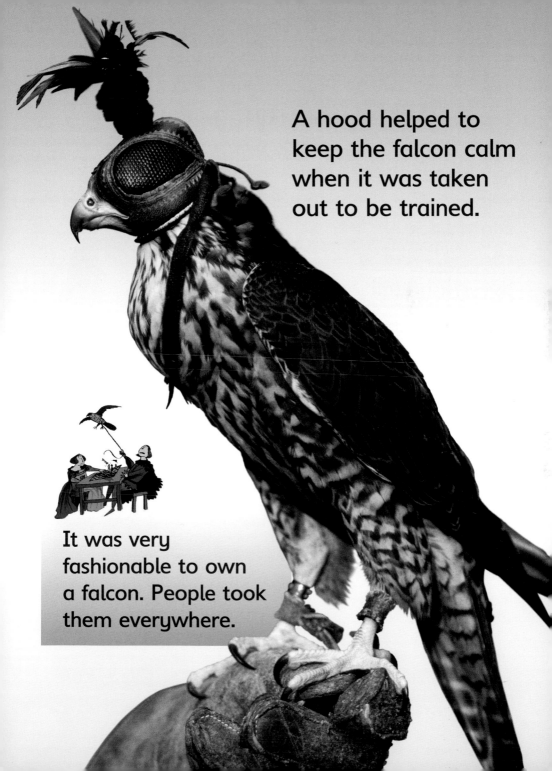

A hood helped to keep the falcon calm when it was taken out to be trained.

It was very fashionable to own a falcon. People took them everywhere.

# In the kitchen

The kitchen was a building in the castle grounds. All the meals were made there.

Meat was roasted over a fire, on a stick called a spit.

This is how part of a castle kitchen might have looked.

1. To bake bread, bakers lit a fire in an oven to heat it up.

2. They mixed dough for bread and made it into loaves.

3. The loaves went in the oven when the fire died down.

4. The oven was still hot, so the bread soon cooked.

Castles didn't have refrigerators, so food went bad quickly. Cooks added spices to disguise the horrible taste.

# Fabulous feasts

Huge meals called feasts were served in the Great Hall of the castle.

Important guests sat at a high table.

Everyone else sat on long benches.

There were no forks in castle times. People usually ate with their fingers.

People ate lots
of meat and fish.

Cooks decorated food
with feathers and fruit.

Amazing models made of sugar and paper
were carried in to impress the guests.

19

# Knights

Knights were rich, important soldiers.
They helped to protect castles
against enemies.

Knights had
shapes or pictures
on their shields.
Each knight had
his own pattern.

First a knight put on a thick, padded vest.

Over this he wore a shirt made of metal.

Metal plates covered his arms, legs and chest.

Then he put on a long top and big gloves.

He wore a heavy metal helmet on his head.

He carried a wooden shield to protect him.

# At a joust

A joust was a pretend fight between two knights.

The knights held long poles called lances.

They rode on strong horses called chargers.

The winner of a joust got a prize. Sometimes he won the losing knight's horse and weapons.

The two knights charged up to each other, on a narrow track.

Each knight tried to push the other one off his horse with a lance.

The knight who was able to stay on his horse was the winner.

# Attack!

Sometimes castles were attacked. Enemies often used a machine called a catapult.

1. Soldiers pulled a big lever back.

2. They loaded it with heavy rocks.

3. Then they let the lever spring up.

4. The rocks hit the castle walls.

Enemies often catapulted dead animals into castles, to spread diseases.

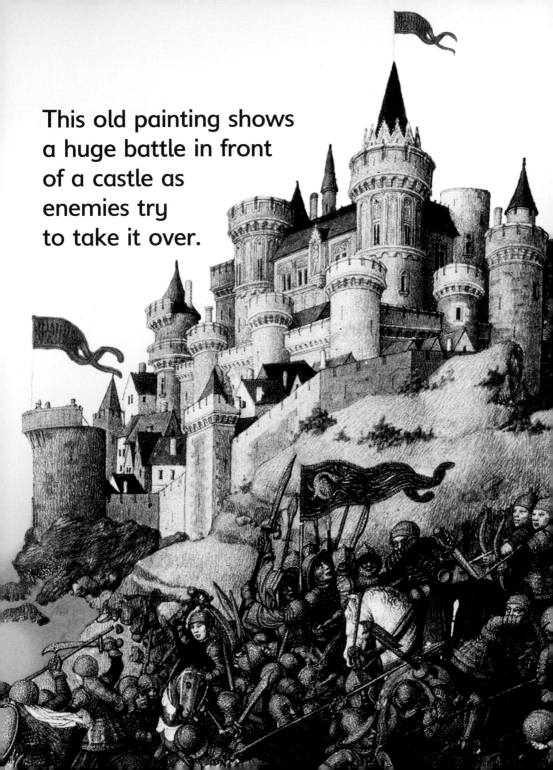

This old painting shows a huge battle in front of a castle as enemies try to take it over.

# Fighting back

Soldiers tried to keep their castle safe from enemies.

They dropped rocks or boiling water onto the heads of enemies who came near.

Sometimes enemies tried to sneak into castles in disguise.

The soldiers were armed with bows and sharp arrows.

They fired arrows through thin slits in the wall.

This castle has many arrow slits in its walls. Soldiers also shot arrows from the roof.

# Castles in ruins

Most castles are now empty. They have crumbled over the years.

This is how Raglan Castle, in Wales, might have looked 400 years ago.

This is how the castle looks now.

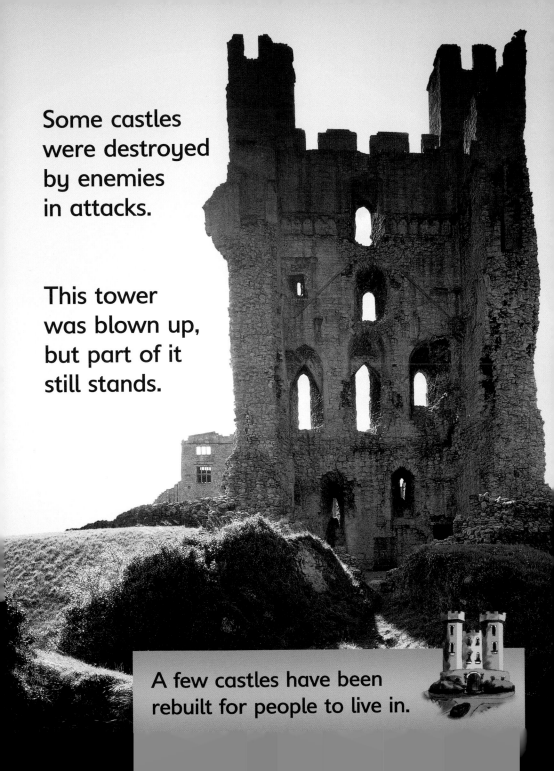

Some castles were destroyed by enemies in attacks.

This tower was blown up, but part of it still stands.

A few castles have been rebuilt for people to live in.

# Glossary of castle words

Here are some of the words in this book you might not know. This page tells you what they mean.

 keep - the main tower of a castle. It usually had a wall around it.

 drawbridge - a bridge that was pulled up to keep enemies out of a castle.

 falcon - a type of large bird. Falcons can be trained to hunt smaller birds.

 feast - a huge meal for lots of people, with plenty to eat and drink.

 shield - a tough, wooden plate. Knights used shields to protect themselves.

 joust - a game where two knights tried to knock each other off their horses.

 catapult - a machine that could fling rocks and other things through the air.

# Websites to visit

You can visit exciting websites to find out more about castles. For links to sites with video clips and activities, go to the Usborne Quicklinks website at **www.usborne.com/quicklinks** and type in the keywords "**beginners castles**".

Always ask an adult before using the internet and make sure you follow these basic rules:

1. Never give out personal information, such as your name, address, school or telephone number.

2. If a website asks you to type in your name or email address, check with an adult first.

The websites are regularly reviewed and the links at Usborne Quicklinks are updated. However, Usborne Publishing is not responsible and does not accept liability for the content or availability of any website other than its own. We recommend that children are supervised while on the internet.

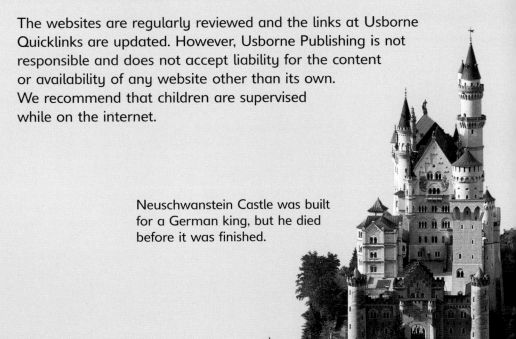

Neuschwanstein Castle was built for a German king, but he died before it was finished.

# Index

acrobats, 12
bedrooms, 8, 10
bows and arrows, 27
catapult, 24, 30
chapel, 8
drawbridge, 7, 30
falcons, 14-15, 30
feasts, 18-19, 30
fighting, 24-25, 26-27, 29
food, 9, 16, 17, 18, 19
Great Hall, 8, 18
guard room, 9
hunting, 14-15
jesters, 12

jousts, 22-23, 30
jugglers, 12
keep, 5, 6, 8-9, 30
kitchen, 9, 16-17
knights, 20-21, 22-23
moat, 7
musicians, 12, 13
rats, 9
ruined castles, 28-29
servants, 4, 10, 11
shields, 20, 21, 30
soldiers, 4, 24, 25, 26, 27
storeroom, 9
wooden castles, 6

## Acknowledgements

Photographic manipulation by Emma Julings
With thanks to Grace Bryan-Brown and The National Trust for the model on page 19.

**Photo credits**
The publishers are grateful to the following for permission to reproduce material:
**Cover** © Tim Gartside/ Robert Harding Picture Library; **p1** © The Bridgeman Art Library/Bibliotheque Royale de Belgique, Brussels, Belgium; **p2-3** © Photononstop/Superstock; **p6** © Gary Cralle/Getty Images; **p7** © Mike Morton/E & E Picture Library; **p10** © Leeds Castle (Angelo Hornak); **p13** © Lebrecht Collection; **p15** © Yann Arthus-Bertrand/Corbis; **p16** Crown copyright: Historic Royal Palaces; **p20** Crown Copyright CADW: Welsh Historic Monuments; **p22** © Pete Dancs/Getty Images; **p25** © Historical Picture Archive/Corbis; **p27** © Corbis/Araldo de Luca; **p28** © Chris Bland; Eye Ubiquitous/Corbis; **p29** © English Heritage Photo Library; **p31** © Ric Ergenbright/Corbis.

Every effort has been made to trace and acknowledge ownership of copyright. If any rights have been omitted, the publishers offer to rectify this in any subsequent editions following notification.

This edition first published in 2015 by Usborne Publishing Ltd., Usborne House, 83-85 Saffron Hill, London EC1N 8RT, England. www.usborne.com Copyright © 2015, 2006, 2003 Usborne Publishing Ltd. The name Usborne and the devices ♀ ⊕ are Trade Marks of Usborne Publishing Ltd. All rights reserved. No part of this publication may be reproduced, stored in a retrieval system, or transmitted in any form or by any means, electronic, mechanical, photocopying, recording or otherwise without the prior permission of the publisher.
First published in America 2015. U.E.